MALACHY DOYLE was born in Northern Ireland and studied psychology before becoming a secondary school teacher in Leeds. After several years in advertising, he returned to education to work in schools for children with special needs. Now a full-time children's author, he has written over 30 books. His *Tales from Old Ireland* (Barefoot Books) won a Parents' Choice Award in the USA. His books for Frances Lincoln include *Babies Like Me!* and *Una and the Sea-Cloak*.

CHRISTINA BRETSCHNEIDER trained as a painter in Düsseldorf, but then discovered she wanted to be an illustrator. She went to Hamburg and graduated with a Masters in Design. Christina lives in the beautiful city of Potsdam in Germany with her two cats, and has become a very keen sailor on the lakes surrounding the city. She regularly contributes illustrations to newspapers and magazines in Germany. This is her first book for Frances Lincoln.

Oh, I'd never be without you, Lizzie Bee   M.D.
For my parents, thank you so much!   C.B.

Teddybear Blue copyright © Frances Lincoln Limited 2004
Text copyright © Malachy Doyle 2004
Illustrations copyright © Christina Bretschneider 2004

The right of Malachy Doyle to be identified as the Author
of this work has been asserted by him in accordance with
the Copyright, Designs and Patents Act, 1988.

First published in Great Britain in 2004 by
Frances Lincoln Children's Books, 4 Torriano Mews,
Torriano Avenue, London NW5 2RZ
www.franceslincoln.com

First paperback edition published
in Great Britain in 2006.

Distributed in the USA by Publishers Group West

British Library Cataloguing in Publication
Data available on request

ISBN 10: 1-84507-126-3
ISBN 13: 978-184507-126-4

Printed in Singapore

1 3 5 7 9 8 6 4 2

Visit the Malachy Doyle website at
www.malachydoyle.co.uk

Teddybear Blue

Written by Malachy Doyle

Illustrated by

Christina Bretschneider

F

FRANCES LINCOLN
CHILDREN'S BOOKS

First thing in the morning
he's the one I want to cuddle,
but he's always up before me
and he's hiding in a huddle.
It's the Mummy-Daddy-help-me-
find-my-teddybear blues.

Now you see him,
now you don't.
Now you'll find him,
now you won't.

Now you've got
the disappearing
teddybear blues.

At ten o'clock

we're in the park,

but Teddy's lurking

in the dark.

oh, please will someone
find for me
a teddybear who's...

not always disappearing
when I want him by my side.
Not always running off somewhere

and playing
hidey-hide.

A teddybear who's good,
and not a teddybear who's not.
Not a teddybear who's giving me
the **teddybear blueS.**

Yet I **love** him, more than all my other toys put together.

When I'm sad he **always** finds me
and, good or bad, whatever,
he snuggles up beside me
and there's nothing more to do.
Oh, I'd never be without you,

Teddy Blue.

You're the one I always choose,
you're the one I hate to lose,

from your fliffy-fluffy haircut
to your funny little shoes.

And that's why we're always singing
when we settle down to snooze,
the one-and-only, never lonely,
teddybear blues.

Oh, I know I say I'll give you
to my sister, **but I don't.**
I know I say I'll find
another teddy,
but I won't.

Because even though you're naughty
when you run away and hide,
there's no one in the world
that I would rather have beside
me in the middle of the night
when I am lonely,
only you.

My now-you-see-me,
now-you-don't,
**Teddybear
Blue.**

OTHER TITLES FROM FRANCES LINCOLN CHILDREN'S BOOKS

UNA AND THE SEA-CLOAK

Malachy Doyle

Illustrated by Alison Jay

Martin can't believe his eyes when a strange girl
staggers out of the sea. "How can I go home now
my sea-cloak is in tatters?" she cries. Martin and
his mother decide to help Una to repair
her sea-cloak, but it is no easy task.

ISBN 1-84507-082-8

EDDIE'S GARDEN

Sarah Garland

Eddie works hard in his garden – digging,
pulling up the weeds and watering his plants.
Soon the garden looks wonderful, full of
tasty treats that will make his picnic with
Lily, Mum and Grandad the best one ever!

ISBN 1-84507-089-5

YUCK!

Mick Manning and Brita Granström

What's for supper? A wriggly worm? YUCK!
Come and join all sorts of babies in the slimiest,
stinkiest, most revolting feast ever. But with spiders,
lizards and rotten eggs on the menu,
who will say YUM! and who will say YUCK!

ISBN 1-84507-423-8

Frances Lincoln titles are available from all good bookshops.
You can also buy books and find out more about your favourite titles,
authors and illustrators at our website: www.franceslincoln.com